The Story of Lilly & Lou
Based on a true story

by
Doriane Lucia, M.Ed.

CCB Publishing
British Columbia, Canada

The Story of Lilly & Lou: Based on a true story

Copyright ©2008 by Doriane Lucia
ISBN-13   978-0-9809995-4-9
First Edition

Library and Archives Canada Cataloguing in Publication

Lucia, Doriane
The Story of Lilly & Lou: based on a true story / story by Doriane Lucia;
[illustrated by Anthony T. DeVito].
Also available in electronic format.
ISBN 978-0-9809995-4-9
1. Dogs--Juvenile fiction. I. DeVito, Anthony T. II. Title.
III. Title: Story of Lilly and Lou.
PZ10.3.L964St 2008   j813'.6   C2008-903205-5

Editor: Lori Ada Jaroslow – www.loriadajaroslow.com
Illustrator: Anthony T. DeVito – www.atdillustration.com

This book is printed on acid free paper derived from new growth trees.

Publisher: CCB Publishing
             British Columbia, Canada
             www.ccbpublishing.com

To Mick, Sadie & Bula
with Love and Gratitude

Special thanks to my mother, sister, niece, nephews, cousin and friends, not only for their love and support, but for letting me use their names even though there may not have been any character connection.

Thank you Paul Rabinovitch of CCB Publishing for making this dream a reality, for believing in this story and appreciating the importance of Humane Education.

Heartfelt thanks *to* ...

The amazing group of people in New York City who helped rescue Mick and Sadie, continued to care about them and changed my life and their lives forever;

My mother, sister, family and friends for supporting my Humane Education mission and my late father for showing me the importance of understanding and respecting animals and for showing me that a true pack leader never needs to intimidate or hit an animal and that strong men do cry when their dog passes away.

To the earth angels (some of my dearest friends) who continually and courageously help animals in need, spending their hard-earned money teaching me more about compassion every day and never make me explain what brings me joy...they just get it and to the Animal Control Officers who go above and beyond to truly make a difference;

Lori for helping me bring this story to life and making it easier for me to relive it during the editing process, Tony for his creativity and talent, and especially to Paul Rabinovitch of CCB Publishing for his expertise and guidance, for making this dream a reality and for believing in this story and appreciating the importance of Humane Education;

Every animal who has blessed my life teaching me some of life's most important lessons;

And finally thank you to everyone who tries to make this world a brighter place especially when no-one is looking.

FOREWORD

The Story of Lilly & Lou is captivating, heartwarming, and instructive. Doriane Lucia has written a story that children (and adults) will adore. At the same time, we all learn to care a bit more because of Lilly and Lou.

Zoe Weil
May 2007

Zoe Weil is the President of the Institute for Humane Education and author of *Above All, Be Kind, Most Good, Least Harm* and two children's books, *Claude and Medea: The Hellburn Dogs* and *So, You Love Animals*.

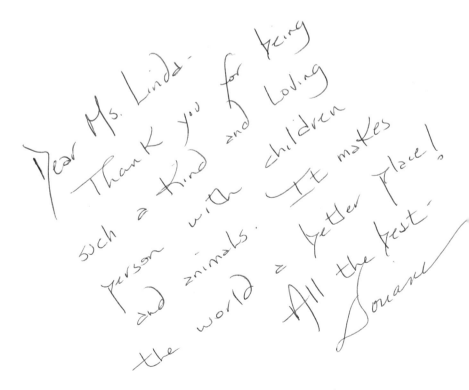

Dear Ms. Linda -
Thank you for being such a kind and loving person with the children and animals. It makes the world a better place!
All the best -
Doriane

August 2011

Part of me knows it's time to get up and start the day and the other part of me hopes that this is just another dream. Maybe it's really Saturday. My head feels heavy with sleepiness. I'm not sure if I can lift it off the pillow. One eyelid tries to hoist itself up so I can see the clock on the nightstand. Just as the neon numbers come into focus telling me that it's 6:15 a.m., I feel a cold, wet nudge against my arm and I sense two eyes staring at me. How did she hear my eye open?

I finally manage to open both eyes and I see that Lilly has her front legs on the bed, and she's stretching her little body as far as she can. My dog Lilly has a black muzzle with some gray in it and brownish, red fur on the rest of her petite body. She has huge, pensive brown eyes. Lilly practices yoga upon awakening. This morning her eyes seem to say… *I've gone outside and taken care of business myself, I did The Downward Facing Dog, and I've been waiting patiently since 6:00 a.m., so do you think you could please GET UP ALREADY? We need to see what's going on out in the world. Come on, Alicia, carpe diem; let's seize the day.*

By now, Lilly's brother Lou has joined the morning ritual. Lilly and Lou look almost identical except that Lou is twice as big as Lilly. They both have thick fur and curly tails. I run my hand through Lou's coat and in my fogginess I reach for my

1

jeans, slide them on, throw on a tee shirt, grab both leashes, yell to Mom that I'm leaving and we're off. I get to look at the tall trees against the clear sky. When Lilly and Lou sniff each morning it's like they're getting the morning news. If I pull them away mid-sniff, it would be like someone yanking a book out of my hand just as I get to the good part. I can almost see Lilly thinking, *Hmmm, smells like the huge white poodle has been by.* Now Lou runs over to get a whiff.

We go a few more yards when Lilly stops in her tracks for another sniff story. This one takes her awhile to decipher. She sniffs more and more, leading us further up the road. I think I know what's going on in Lilly and Lou's heads or maybe I'm superimposing my own thoughts on them. The important thing is that I know enough about dogs to know what they need each day. Suddenly, that cute puppy, Duke, comes our way with the guy who acts like he's walking a tiger. There is a huge choke chain around the cheerful little puppy, and the guy tugs him and shouts orders. "Sit. Stay. Heal." Just as Duke is getting a good sniff and trying to greet us, the drill sergeant yanks the dog away and doesn't let us visit. But Duke always seems hopeful that one day he'll get to stop and play with us. Both Lilly and Lou look at me and I imagine they are thinking … *we love our life.*

The three of us venture to Aroma Café. My mom lets me get breakfast there two times a week and today is our day. We love Aroma Café. Everyone there is so friendly to me and especially to my canine companions. We enter my favorite patio area where bougainvillea is bursting with bright pink flowers.

There is always a table filled with people who work on movies. There's a nice teenage girl named Cynthia with long brown hair who always says hi to me. She told me she's an intern working with her brother Howie who is a really cool camera man. He rides his motorcycle here. Then there's a lady with jet black hair, usually wearing big hoop earrings and colorful makeup. Actually, she is a hairstylist and makeup artist for actors and then there's an older man who looks like the director of the group. They always have someone new sitting with them. It's like an early morning club. Lilly and Lou have become very popular with this group so I make sure to pass by so that everyone can pet and greet them. "Hi, Lou. Hi, Lilly," they chime in like a chorus. Finally, someone says, "Oh, hey, Alicia. How's it going?" I feel like a special part of their club. Lilly and Lou love Aroma because everyone dotes on them.

As usual, Aroma is jammed. At first glance, there are no tables available. While I'm putting in my order, I see a table for two open up and I grab it. As I'm waiting for my number to be called so I can pick up my food, a lady walks towards me. When it's crowded, strangers at Aroma will share tables. This woman is wearing an enormous lime green hat. The rim is so big; I think a flock of birds might build a nest on it. Her lips are bright red and shiny, and she's wearing a dress with big flowers on it. I can't figure out if she is talking to herself or singing. I wonder if she's a little crazy or maybe just eccentric. I wonder if she is some over the top actress. The thought repeats in my head. *Please don't let her sit at my table; please don't let her sit with me…* She walks right past the movie people and clearly has her sights set on the empty chair at my table. What if people think she's my mother or my friend? I look to see if the cool movie people are looking at me. I smile at them and see them laughing. I wonder if they're laughing at me.

I hear my mother's voice in my head. "Alicia, don't judge a book by its cover." Now, her voice is getting louder inside my head. "Remember how judgmental people were when your father had to wear that neck brace after his car accident? They weren't very nice and you didn't like it at all."

Suddenly I was snapped back into the present when bird head lady moved right next to my table. I looked at my book and feigned interest when suddenly I heard a proper English accent. "Oh what beeaaauuutiful dogs you have. *Wow, I didn't know there were so many vowels in the word beautiful.* "What kind are they, love?"

"I really don't know," I tell her, "maybe Shepherd mixes. I found them in a park in New York City." The lady's cherry red lips press together tightly and her forehead crinkles up. "Did you say you found them in New York City?" she said, puzzled.

"This is the only empty seat in the house. Do you mind if I sit here?" *Do I really have a choice ...* I thought to myself ... *I wish you would sit anywhere other than here.* But she seemed like a decent person and she expressed interest in the two beings in my life besides my mom and dad, who are closest to my heart, my dogs Lilly and Lou. *I better take my mom's advice...* I thought and then said aloud, "Sure," trying to hide my discomfort. She sat down and sipped her latte.

"My name is Ina. Can you tell me more about these sweet looking and very well-behaved dogs?"

I extended my hand to her. "Hi, my name's Alicia. Well, do you know New York City at all?" I asked.

She smiled as if my question made her happy. "Actually, I

do. I moved here to Los Angeles from the Upper West Side of Manhattan about five years ago."

"Wow," I said. "My mom, dad and I used to live on the Upper West Side too!"

I had never heard someone say no quite like this lady. "Noooooooo, what block?" she asked.

"Ninety-Seventh and Central Park West."

She started to laugh. "My darling, I lived on Ninety-Fifth Street and Central Park West. I probably walked right past you on more than one occasion. Did your parents live there for a long time before you moved here?"

"After my parents got married and decided to live in Manhattan, they looked at apartments, but they were very expensive. My dad was a Professor at NYU and my mom was going to school for her Master's degree in social work. They were excited when they found our apartment because the building had subsidized housing for people who didn't make a ton of money."

Ina nodded. "Yes, I remember when those buildings turned into condos and got doormen and fancy lobbies. Your parents were lucky. While I loved that they revitalized Central Park and made those buildings look nicer, they also converted one of New York City's best jazz clubs, *McHales*, into a drab eating establishment."

I laughed and said, "My parents complained about that too!"

5

"So, please continue. You said you found these dogs in the park?" she asked.

"Some lady threw them out of her car."

"My heavens. I've never heard of such a thing. How awful that a person would abandon their pets in such a manner."

I see Lilly and Lou hunker down and get comfortable, and they both look like they're rolling their eyes and thinking ... *Oh boy, here she goes again, she's going to tell this lady the whole doggoned story about us, get that lost look in her eyes likes she's in some sort of trance, get sad, then happy and then she'll be rushing to get to school... again.*

Every time I start telling the story of Lilly and Lou, I feel as though it happened yesterday. I begin to tell Ina what happened...

The morning of February 3rd I could not wait to get to Riverside Park with my dog Bella. It had just snowed again and I knew that Bella would love to play in the snow. Even though we were right next to Central Park, I liked Riverside Park better. It reminded me of the country. Since we didn't have a country house, I would pretend that the park was the backyard of our country cabin.

I loved the blanket of snow that covered all the trees, the old fashioned lamp posts and the view of the Hudson River. But what I especially liked about Riverside Park were the people. There were so many people who let their dogs run and play safely; away from other people.

I always feel sad when I talk about Bella because she died

not too long ago from a condition she had her whole life. But it makes me smile to think that my Doberman Boxer mix, Bella, was rescued from a junkyard in the Bronx. We had so much fun together despite her medical problems. She had short hair and would shiver if she got too cold. But it didn't stop her from wanting to go out and play in the snow. We bought her a fleece jacket to keep her warm and cozy. She was always ready to romp.

Bella would get so excited watching the snow fly up in the air as she jumped in it. I would throw snowballs and she seemed confused when she tried to catch them. The snowballs would fall apart in her mouth unlike the firm toy balls she could hold in her muzzle.

We were having a great time. It was a perfect February day like many we had had before. Suddenly, out of nowhere I noticed two dogs running aimlessly through the snow. I looked around to see who they belonged to, but nobody was close by. I saw a woman walking briskly ahead of me. She was bundled up in a coat that looked like a sleeping bag with a hood. Her face was down to protect it from the wind. I caught up with her and asked her if she knew who the dogs belonged to. She said rather sharply that she had no idea and then picked up her pace even more.

I tried another person. "Excuse me sir, but do you know who those two dogs belong to?" I asked.

"Sorry," he replied, "I've never seen them before."

I started to worry because nobody seemed to care about these stray dogs. The cold snapped at my face as I ran around trying to get people to stop long enough to answer my question. People in New York City tend to walk quickly but on that day, everyone seemed to be speeding to their destinations because it was about to snow again. I couldn't understand why nobody seemed concerned. I looked back to where I had first seen the dogs. They were gone. I turned and looked everywhere. I ran here and there, spinning and looking and rubbing tears off my face with my mittens. So many thoughts ran through my head, like, where could they go in this freezing cold and were they lost or did they run away from home and why didn't they have collars on. It was starting to get dark and I knew my mother would be worried if Bella and I didn't get home soon. There was nobody left in the park. I strained and looked everywhere when in the distance I saw one last person. He was far away, and I probably wouldn't have seen him if he hadn't been wearing a puffy, orange parka and a striped scarf that was wrapped around his head and neck. I picked up my pace to reach him.

At this point Bella looked like she had had it and I'm sure she would have preferred to return to the warm apartment, but I insisted she pick up the pace.

"Bella, don't forget your puppyhood. These dogs need help just like you did when I first met you. We have to help them."

Bella walked faster and I knew she understood. Because people were so disinterested up to this point, I was shy and scared to talk to the guy with the striped scarf.

As I got closer to him, I realized that it was my mom and dad's friend Brendan who lives in my building. He's a funny guy and is always beatboxing so I gave him a stage name.

"Mista B, I'm so glad to see you."

"Hey, Alicia. How are you doing?"

"There are two dogs running around the park who have brownish red fur. One is small and the other medium sized. Have you seen them or do you know their story? They don't look like they belong to anyone."

Brendan stared at me with his kind, misty green eyes. I'd never seen him sad before. He said, "Those dogs have been out here for days."

I shook my head in disbelief and rattled off questions faster than he could answer me. "How could that be? How can they stand this freezing cold weather? Are they lost? Has anyone tried to catch them?"

We walked together while he told me what he knew.

"Last week my friend Keith was in the park with his dogs when out of nowhere this lady drives by the edge of the park on 115th Street, opens the door, throws the dogs out and speeds away."

I was shocked. "Did anyone get her license plate number?" I asked in disbelief.

"Nope, unfortunately not. Keith was so worried about the dogs that he barely gave the car another glance. He had almost no information to give to an Animal Control Officer. The only thing he noticed was that she had out of state plates. Keith chased after the dogs the minute she let them out of her car. He was calling after them and trying to catch them."

"Did anyone call the animal shelter to try and help catch the dogs?" I asked.

"Yeah, but some folks were not too happy about that. Besides, I don't know if the Animal Control Officers would be able to spend this much time tracking the dogs like we are."

I listened and thought that there is a lot of stuff that I just don't understand.

"What did Keith do when he saw the dogs get released from the car?"

"Well, he called after the dogs and tried to follow them but they looked scared and would run when he got close."

"Wait," I said, "these dogs have been outside in this sub-zero weather for a week now?"

"Yup," he answered, "and we don't know what to do."

"We?" I asked. "Who's we?"

He continued, "A group of regular people who come here with their dogs have been trying to catch these dogs for the past week."

"Brendan," I shouted, "there they are!" They were about one hundred feet away from us. I bent down and spoke to them in a sweet voice. I told them I wouldn't hurt them.

"Hey, Alicia," Brendan said, "watch. They're terrified of people but when Bella gets next to the little red dogs – oh, that's what we call them, the little red dogs – they let her get close to them. They're comfortable with strange dogs but not with people."

"No wonder they're scared of people," I said. "They must have had a pretty crummy life with that woman if she could abandon them like that. Now what, Brendan?"

"Well, since the animal shelter has not come to catch them, we're trying to catch them ourselves."

At that point, all we could see were pools of light on the ground coming from the streetlights. We could barely see two feet in front of us, let alone see the two little red dogs.

"This is really upsetting," I said.

"I know, Alicia, I feel it too," said Brendan. "I'm sure some folks will be out again tomorrow to try to catch them. By the way, it looks like the medium sized dog is a boy and the little one is a girl. Maybe they're brother and sister."

I thought maybe they were mother and son. Either way, we both agreed that they were definitely best friends.

Brendan nodded. "For sure. I'm going to stay in the park a while longer. You better head home. Stay strong, Alicia."

"Thanks, Mista B, I'll try."

As Bella and I walked away, I gave her a full body hug, and

then burst into tears. I'm not sure why I cried. I guess I felt sad, mad at the woman who left the dogs, helpless and frustrated all at the same time.

It was even colder now that the sun had gone down and I was starving. But I knew that in ten minutes, we could walk inside a warm apartment and have a nice, hot meal. I was afraid that the two red dogs might not make it through the night. It could have been a week since they had eaten anything.

When I got home, I told Mom that Brendan was in the park and that he was concerned about the dogs too.

"Oh yes," she said, "that makes sense. I remember Brendan mentioning that he works with a wonderful animal rescue group. He's a good person."

My mom gave Brendan a call to make sure he would keep an eye on me. Even though Dad taught me a lot about dogs, Mom reminded me that I was not allowed to actually catch the dogs. Even though they looked sweet, they could bite me out of fear. She was okay with me going with Brendan if he would be the one to catch them. She tried to cheer me up about the dogs by putting on a funny movie, but I kept thinking about them being out in the park cold, hungry and alone with just each other. I prayed that the next day we could catch them.

Luckily, the next day was Saturday and I didn't have to be anywhere in the morning. I was on a mission and asked Mom if I could go see if Brendan was in the park already. Without saying a word, she pulled out Bella's coat, put it on her, gave me a hug and said, "Good luck. Please come home soon and call me if you need help."

I thanked her and blew her a kiss. Bella and I were off. I was focused on going straight to the park. Bella and I had done this walk so many times before but today the five long blocks from Central Park West to Riverside Park seemed like fifty million miles. We finally made it to Riverside Drive.

We walked a few blocks uptown to get to the long staircase that leads down into the park. Just as I put my foot on the first step to go down into the park, I heard a loud truck horn blasting. I looked at the road to see what was going on. There they were! A big green pickup truck almost hit the boy dog. The man in the truck yelled, "Get out of the road, you stupid dogs. Then he looked straight at me and yelled, "You idiot, put leashes on those dogs. What's wrong with you?"

My heart practically popped out of my coat as I watched them run toward the busy street. They were trying to stay close to each other but it was hard with cars whizzing past them. I was scared they'd get hit. They were headed in the direction that I had just come from and were going away from the park, not toward it! They ran right past "Café con Leche," my favorite Spanish restaurant where the sweet smells spilled onto the street inviting us to come in. I wanted to get them food so badly, but I couldn't take my eyes off them for a second. The smells wafting over the corner of Ninety-Sixth Street and Broadway must have tortured them. I thought maybe I could at least coax them off the street and back into the park but they kept going the opposite way. They crossed West End Avenue, Broadway, Amsterdam and then Columbus Avenue. I ran behind them calling, "Come on little dogs, please come to me. I promise I won't hurt you. Please come to me." At the same time I was calling them, I was afraid I might scare them back into the road again so I walked slowly behind them.

They headed towards a big dumpster and started sniffing around for food that may have dropped to the ground. There was nothing for them but even if they had found something, it probably would have been frozen. Then I saw a boy who looked like he was around eleven years old coming around the corner. The boy dog got very close to the young boy. The kid started laughing and teasing the dogs and making loud barking sounds. He shouted, "Hey, dumb dogs, go eat something at home." He picked up a rock and threw it at them but luckily it missed them. I was mad but I didn't have time to talk to the boy because the dogs ran off into the street and almost got hit again. I kept walking behind the dogs. Before I knew it they had reached Central Park.

I was scared because Central Park is bigger than Riverside Park. Whenever I went there with Bella it seemed like a lot of the people without dogs weren't nice to people with dogs. I was afraid that if they saw the two lost dogs, they may not be nice to them. Also, this park goes all the way over to the east side of the city. I was hoping that someone would help. I couldn't believe it. Just at that moment, I looked up and saw my friend Leslie. She already graduated from high school but we were still friends. She was walking her purebred Boxer named Calvin that her parents purchased for her from a dog breeder. She named him Calvin because she likes Calvin Klein clothes. I liked her and her dog a lot. I never told her this, but I wish she had gone to a Boxer rescue organization to adopt a dog.

"Hey, Leslie," I said.

"Alicia, what's up? You look upset."

I told her about the dogs and asked for her help. She said

that she had to go home for lunch and besides it was too cold to stay out another minute.

She continued, "I'm sorry I can't help, Alicia, but don't let this upset you so much. There are people who don't have enough to eat in New York and homeless people who need help too."

I felt like she was saying this shouldn't be so important to me. My mother always told me that there are a lot of big problems in the world and it wouldn't be good if we all cared about the same things. Besides, she'd tell me, it's just not good to judge someone for caring about something that you don't get involved in. "Compassion is contagious," my mom would say.

I was kind of disappointed with Leslie but I bit my tongue. I wanted to ask her if she cared about anything other than designer clothes. Instead I said, "Thanks anyway, Leslie, right now I need to find someone who will help me." As I walked off, I turned around and called to her, "Oh, hey, Leslie, there's a homeless guy on the corner of Broadway and Ninety–Sixth Street. He wears a purple corduroy hat and a blue pea coat. He loves cheese sandwiches, no mayo and a large hot chocolate."

I kept looking for the little red dogs, but no luck.

I had a rehearsal in a little while for *Shout about It,* an original musical theatre piece that we were putting on at school. I knew I would need to concentrate that night and not worry about the dogs. I would have to stay focused. The director would be finalizing the blocking of the show. This was one of the best public schools in New York City for theatre. I worked hard to audition for the theatre group three years ago when I was thirteen and was excited that I had gotten in. I didn't want to mess things up now. When I got to rehearsal, I told my fellow cast members about the dogs. They were shocked and many of them offered to help. It was great that they cared about the situation, which made it easier for me to concentrate during rehearsal.

When I got home that night I went straight to bed so I could get an early start on my search the next morning. When I went to the kitchen for breakfast, my mother said she could hear me talking in my sleep. She came into my room and heard me say, "Come on little pups, please come to me." She said I was tossing and turning. I was pretty beat on Sunday morning because I didn't get much sleep but I knew a second wind of determination would kick in.

My mother didn't want me going to the park alone again so she called Brendan to see if he was heading there. The weather report said it was going to snow again, so I bundled up and met Brendan in the lobby. He had been working late the night before and looked like he was sleepwalking. He mumbled, "First stop, Ms. Alicia, is the coffee shop."

"You sure you're going to make it Mista B?"

All he could do was nod. Once Brendan was coffee'd up and more alert, we headed to Riverside Park. I looked at Bella with her new winter coat on. Brendan smiled, looked at me and then at Bella and said, "Come on, girls, we've got work to do."

We hoped the pups would be there. We both agreed that even though it was cold, at least it was a beautiful, sunny day.

Brendan asked about Bella and commented on how well she walked with us. I told him about my parent's friend Bob who is an awesome positive reinforcement trainer who helped me with Bella.

"By any chance, does he do a lot of work with abused pit bulls?"

"Yeah, do you know him?"

"No, but I've heard of him. He's really into helping animals and a very cool guy."

I asked Brendan when he thought he would get another dog.

"When I rescued Jackson, I wasn't working so many hours. But after he passed away, I started working a lot more. It wouldn't be fair to a dog, especially a puppy to have to be alone that much. When I have any extra time I volunteer with rescue groups and as often as possible I do what we're doing right now."

"That's cool, Brendan," I replied.

As we entered the park, Brendan and I couldn't believe our eyes. Right in front of us were the two little red dogs. They were so close to us I wanted to scream with excitement. Instead I called to them. I gently put my hand in my pocket ready to grab the leashes I had just in case and handed them to Brendan. Both dogs stopped and for a split second we thought they might come to us.

The boy looked right at me. Then the girl did too. I wondered what she was thinking. Seeing the sadness in their eyes tore me up. They both looked exhausted and like they really wanted to trust someone but there was also terror in their big brown eyes. Brendan walked very slowly so they could barely tell that he was moving. There was a fence right in front of us, and I thought they were trapped.

He moved toward the little girl but she was so skinny from not eating that she slipped right through the slats in the fence. The boy dog ran down the path to the end of the fencing and caught up with the girl. They both scurried away down into the park. We missed them by inches.

My excitement turned to a feeling of helplessness again and my breakfast turned to lead in my stomach. We just looked at each other, shrugged our shoulders and sighed. As we turned to walk away, we saw a guy coming towards us wearing a crazy fluorescent colored hat and scarf, and glasses that looked like ski goggles. He was walking with a group of five dogs, all different shapes and sizes.

Brendan curved his hand around his mouth and shouted, "Hey, Keith!" Brendan introduced us. "Alicia, this is my buddy, Keith. He has also been trying to catch the little guys. Keith, this is Alicia. She's concerned about the dogs too." Keith gave me a "way to go" pat on my shoulder with his huge quilted mitten. I thought I might tip over.

We all walked together and talked. "Wow," I said, "it looks like you have a nice pack of dogs."

"Yeah," he said with a big grin, "I rescued all of them from different places. This is Amsterdam because I found him on Amsterdam Avenue. This is Parker who I found tied to a bench in Central Park. He's named after the musician Charlie Parker, and this is Coltrane after the famous saxophonist, John Coltrane."

Amsterdam, Parker and Coltrane were all big and the others were funny looking little ones. Usually dogs look like their owners and have similar personalities. It was hard to tell which dog Keith was most like.

Bella definitely looked like me. She had the same color hair except for my reddish - purple streaks. Her ears were long like my hair, but I have bangs and her hair was spikier on top. Bella was very protective of people she loved just like I do.

"I had no idea that there were so many homeless and abused dogs until I rescued mine from a junkyard," I told Keith. "I can't believe how careless people can be with animals."

"Keith, Brendan," I shouted, "look, there they are again. They are so skinny. Do you think they'll live much longer?"

Keith and Brendan spoke almost simultaneously and said the same thing. "I hate to say it, Alicia, but I doubt it."

I called ahead to the boy dog. "Come on buddy, please come with us. Look Keith, he's stopping." Then the boy dog stared at us as if he was contemplating a decision with global implications.

"It looks like he's trying to make a choice," I said.

"Yeah, it does," Brendan agreed.

The boy dog took one more look at his partner, then at us. He saw that she had run further away from us and suddenly, he bolted to catch up with her and we could tell that he had made his decision. They ran together again.

They seemed so close; like they knew what the other one was thinking. I let out a long sigh and my breath formed a cloud of smoke from the cold. As we were walking along the path we bumped into a woman and her dog. Adriane was another friend of Keith and Brendan. She and her tiny dog Roxy were also trying to catch the two red dogs. We walked and talked and I learned how she rescued Roxy when she was a little puppy. Roxy had been living in a house where no one took care of her and the kids teased her a lot. Adriane lived next door to them. Roxy escaped one day and when Adriane was not looking Roxy jumped into her car and just sat in the passenger seat and waited for her. They have been together ever since.

I learned that Adriane, as well as other people, were cooking delicious and yummy smelling healthy food for the little red dogs and bringing it to the park to try to lure them. Keith and Adriane shouted in stereo as they saw their friend Lowell up ahead. "Hey Lowell, come on, we're trying to catch the little ones."

Two more friends appeared and Brendan shouted, "Hey, are you here to help us catch the little ones?"

"You bet," one of the guys said, "if we don't get them tonight, they will die. It's going to snow again."

At that point, we all saw the little red dogs darting around the park again. Adriane gasped, "Today the dogs look skinnier than ever and it looks like they can barely walk. They are definitely not walking as quickly as they were a week ago." We all agreed.

A whole group of people including more adults, some kids

and a bigger group of dogs formed a rescue unit and we walked the length of the park determined to save the red dogs. Now we were a team.

I was introduced to Leo, Lee, Nicole and her husband Brian and everyone's dogs, Daisy, Sasha, Ben, Bogie, Devin and Bodie. I stared at Sasha who looked just like Bella. Then I remembered that the lady who rescued Bella told me that a really cool woman from Inwood had rescued Bella's sister.

I said to Nicole, "Hey, by any chance did you get Sasha from Miriam, a woman who rescues dogs? Was Sasha born in a junkyard in the Bronx?"

"Yes!" Nicole shouted. "Are you Alicia?" We both screamed and hugged like we had known each other for years.

"Doesn't that make us in-laws?" Nicole asked.

"I guess so," we both laughed.

"Wow," Nicole noted, "I can't believe you adopted Bella and that she's lived this long. She's big too. Miriam told me that most dogs with her type of problem don't survive."

"I know," I told Nicole. "My dad took me to visit Miriam to see all the dogs she had for adoption. My eyes went right to Bella because she was so cute. She ran, got a ball and gave it to me. She played fetch with me for a long time while my dad talked to Miriam about her condition. By then I really liked this puppy a lot and so did my dad. I could not get her sweet eyes and oversized, floppy ears out of my head. I remember thinking that maybe I was the one who was meant to care for her. We talked it over with my mom and figured out what we would need to do if we adopted her. My mother finally agreed. A couple of days later we picked her up and she never fetched a ball again. She must have been putting on a show for us!" I said, and laughed.

"What was her problem?" Leo asked.

I told him, "Bella was born with a condition called megaesophagus, which means that her esophagus is enlarged and her muscles can't push her food down. It would take us about thirty minutes to feed her three times a day when she was a puppy and now, two times a day. She eats sort of standing up and then has to lay propped up with pillows so the food will go down by gravity. She knows that when we say "time to digest" that it's time to go to the couch and stay propped up for a bit. We made this a happy time for her so she does not try to get up. I think she thinks all dogs eat like this. There are lots of risks with this condition. She had pneumonia twice but we love her a lot and keep a close eye on her. Since we made the decision to adopt her, we'll do whatever it takes to keep her healthy."

Then Nicole said, "This is so cool, we'll be friends for life." You'll have to come up to Connecticut sometime. Brian and I have a farm where we have lots of other rescued animals. I looked up and realized that the entire rescue team had been quietly walking right along side us listening to the story while they kept an eye out for the two dogs. I felt so happy to be with such a great group of people.

Brian brought us back to our mission and shouted, "Let's make a plan."

Keith told us that his sister Anita worked for Channel 5 News and thought maybe we should ask her to do a story about the little red dogs in order to get some extra help.

Brian didn't think that was a good idea. He said by the time the piece was aired, the dogs would be dead. Even though Brian was pretty laid back and fairly quiet, he had an air of confidence and seemed super smart. When he said something, we listened. Everyone agreed that the dogs had to be saved today.

Brendan said, "We called the shelter again but they have not been able to get here yet." Adriane piped in, "Yeah, but they have the skills and equipment to help us."

Brian added, "Yeah, that's true but even if they arrived here right now, I don't know how long they'd be able to stay. I don't think they can be out here after hours, chasing them." It was already 4:30 in the afternoon and it was getting dark.

"I think we just have to think creatively and work together," Brian said.

Right at that moment, we saw the two red dogs searching and circling. We realized they were looking for a place to sleep or bed down as dogs do. It was obvious that they were not only looking for a safe spot but they also needed to stop because they could barely walk. The boy dog almost fell over. They were starving and freezing.

"They must be exhausted," Leo said.

Adriane said, "I think they're going to lie down in the snow and stay put."

The two little dogs found some bushes and hid in them. They laid down so closely to each other in order to keep warm that they looked like one big dog instead of two.

Then Brian took charge of the situation. With certainty he said, "Okay everyone, what we need to do is form a circle and gather around them very slowly. Keith, Brendan and I will take off our jackets and throw them over the dogs to catch them so we don't hurt them or ourselves."

Brendan explained that if the animal shelter was involved, they might use catch poles. This would give them some distance from the dogs and also help protect them from getting bitten.

He continued, "Keith, Brian and I will lead the capture since we are the adults who have the most experience with this." He made me and some others step to the very back of the circle.

We could see the dogs cuddling together in a small ball in the bushes. I don't think they saw us approaching. But when we got close to them, they looked up at us. I saw their wide eyes, fox-like ears and sweet faces more clearly than ever before. They were keeping each other warm and they were motionless. The only thing between us and the dogs were some bushes. My

heart pounded faster and faster and I could see the fear in their eyes as they stared at us.

I wanted desperately for them to understand that we wouldn't hurt them. We approached them very slowly. The circle got smaller and tighter around the dogs. If one of them got up at that point, they would have bumped into us. Suddenly, both dogs jumped up and attempted to make a mad dash. Brian threw his jacket over the boy dog and caught him. Adriane tried to catch the little girl but she slipped right through the circle and ran as fast as she could.

I never imagined I could have so many feelings. I was scared we wouldn't get her, glad we got him, and sad that they were separated even for that minute. Brian held the little boy tightly in his arms. We stayed calm. Brian was gentle with him, hoping he would know that everything would be okay. As the girl ran, she fell down in the snow. She got back up again, took a quick look back at us, and then continued running.

It was almost five o'clock and I had another rehearsal for the musical. This was going to be our technical rehearsal with the lighting and sound guys. We would rehearse all the cues with the tech crew. There would be musicians there and it was going to be a pretty big deal. I would have to put all my thoughts about the dogs aside and trust that my new friends would do whatever needed to be done. But still, the dogs seemed so much more important to me than the play. My new friends assured me they would stay in the park until they caught the little girl. My heart sank as I left everyone in the park and walked home with Bella.

The next morning I got up, took Bella out for a quick walk,

then rushed back home to find out what happened the night before. Everyone must have left for work or school already. I needed to know what happened before I left for school. I dialed one number and got an answering machine, dialed another number and got another machine. I was going nuts. I called one more number. "Hi, this is Alicia. Is this Adriane?"

"Yeah, it is. Hi, Alicia."

I asked her what happened. "I'm going crazy. Did you get the girl dog? Is she okay?" I spoke so quickly I wasn't sure what I was saying.

Adriane began, "Well, we held on to the boy. He's so sweet. The girl was devastated because she was separated from him. Oh, Alicia, this part was terrible. Besides being weak and cold, the little girl was distressed. She was without the partner she had traveled with for weeks. Who knows how long they had been together before we saw them. She thought she lost her best friend and now she was on the street alone. She made gut wrenching sounds howling and crying as she went up and down the park searching for her partner. We decided to put the boy in a crate and then put the crate in the middle of the park pathway. We hated to put him back outside in the cold but we had no choice. We hid in the bushes along the path. We waited and hoped that she would eventually run past the crate. After three long hours of running up and down the park wailing, she discovered he was in the crate. She got so excited that she ran right inside it. She squeezed her skinny little body in between one of the gates to get to him. She snuggled up next to him and whimpered. Then we closed the second door on the crate and brought them to Brendan's house as fast as we could.

I was so happy I was jumping up and down shouting, "They caught the little ones, Bella, they got both of them. Mom, they caught the two red dogs. They're both safe and sound." Bella seemed excited too. I couldn't wait to get to school to tell my fellow cast members.

The first person to take them into their home was Brendan even though he knew he would not be the one to keep them. He said that the dogs were so scared to be with people that they would barely move out of the apartment. While he was at work he had someone come in and check on them. As much as he wanted to keep them, he knew it would not be fair to these little guys.

When I was talking to Adriane one day she gave me an idea. She told me to ask my mom if we could watch them until we found another home for them, and hopefully finding another home would take a really long time. I asked my mom if she would just go over to Brendan's apartment with me so she could see the dogs and consider fostering them. The second my mom saw the dogs she sat down on the ground next to them and said, "I can see why you worked so hard to help these pups. You can see in their eyes how much they have been through and that they need a lot of love."

My mom explained how these pups would need time and consistency with people to build trust, and that Brendan was being kind to the dogs by finding the right place for them. I know that dogs are pack animals by nature, and they shouldn't be left alone for long periods of time, but these dogs needed extra special care. I had already begged my parents to get Bella, so to get permission to keep two more dogs didn't seem likely. I wanted to call my father, who was living in Los Angeles, to see if we could send them to him but that seemed crazy.

The girl dog put her little nose next to my mom's face. My mom put both hands gently around her face and said, "Don't worry little ones we'll take care of you until we find you another good home."

I let out a big sigh, "Oh Mom, thank you, thank you, thank you. I'll come home right after school every day. And I hope you can just help me on the days when I have rehearsals."

"We'll work it out sweetheart," she said and moved on to give the boy dog some attention. She added, "But don't forget, this is temporary."

I told her I understood. Brendan did a little beatboxing and thanked my mom.

"Hey, Alicia, maybe you can come with me next time I go to the shelter. We can go with someone from one of the rescue groups. We're working hard to educate people about animal abuse and pet overpopulation so we can help these animals."

I could tell by the smile on my mom's face that she was definitely open to that idea.

"These two dogs are not the only ones who are on the street or who need help," Brendan continued.

"I think Alicia would love to help out and make a difference," my mom said.

"Hey, Aleesh," Brendan added, "they have junior volunteer

programs. Alicia has what it takes," he said to my mom.

I was definitely excited. "I'm there. Just say when."

Before we left, Mista B assured us that he would do anything he could to help us take care of our new roomies. We took the elevator up to our apartment with the two red dogs and I did my happy dance.

I started to reread all the dog books we had. A lot of them were from when we adopted Bella before my parents separated. My parents were having some problems and right around that time my dad got this great teaching job at UCLA. I miss him a lot but I talk to him practically every day. My father had dogs his whole life so I called him for advice about the little red dogs. I was always happy to hear his voice.

This was his routine. "Is this my favorite child?" he'd say.

"This is your only child!" I'd reply.

Dad was looking forward to us subletting our New York apartment in order to move out west. He was thrilled that my mom landed her dream job as a social worker in Los Angeles, but I think he was especially stoked about the fact that my mom wanted to try to work things out with him. So was I, to say the least.

He asked me the same question each time we talked, "Are you excited to move out here?"

"Of course I am, Daddy. Hey, I need your help. Remember how we never put Bella in a crate? Do you think we need to put these guys in a crate?"

"Based on what you said they've been through, I would use a crate. Let them sleep in your bedroom like Bella does. This will give them what I call 'free bonding time' with you, Alicia. We typically think that we're bonding with our pets when we walk, feed or train them. But while you're sleeping, they'll be able to smell you and feel your presence which will make them feel secure. If they were left with their mom, they would almost never be separated from her or their littermates. But remember, you never want to keep them in the crate for too long. However a perfect time for them to be in their crate is while you are sleeping. Plus, it will let them have space from Bella who by now probably wants them to go back to wherever they came from."

I wondered how my dad knew that.

He continued, "Anything else I can help you with Last Minute Lucy?"

"Very funny, Dad, but I don't wait until the last minute for everything," I replied.

"Uh huh, have you started packing for the move yet?" he asked.

I pretended not to hear him and started humming then said, "Anyway, there's one other thing I need help with. We don't have names for the pups yet. People in the park were coming up with silly names like Lucy and Ricky, Minnie and Mickey, and Fred and Ethel. I wanted to call the boy River and the girl Sundance."

"How about Lou after Lou Reed?" he suggested.

"Oh my gosh," I shouted, "that's what Mom said!"

"He was one of our favorite performers."

I turned the phone away a bit and shouted to my mom, "Guess what Daddy thinks we should call the boy dog, Mom?"

I could hear her laughing. Before they could say Janis after Janis Joplin for the girl dog I said, "Okay, how about Lilly for the girl?"

My dad said, "Lilly and Lou. Perfect, Alicia."

The truth is I was so excited that we were going to be able to keep them, even if it was only for a little while, we could have called them salt and pepper for all I cared. I was just happy that they were safe.

"Thanks. I love you, Dad."

"I love you more Sweet Pea!" he replied.

"See you in a few months."

I gave the dogs lots of time to see that not all people were bad. I needed to earn their trust and never yelled at them. I petted and brushed them very gently every day. I still do. When my mom and I thought that they would be okay going to the vet's office, we brought them to get all their shots, make sure they were healthy and then get spayed and neutered.

I wondered if they would ever trust people. They were getting more comfortable with me, but Lou still seemed scared of some of my friends, especially my friend Paul. When he was around they would barely come out of my bedroom. I wondered if perhaps at some point a man had been really mean to Lou.

One day after school I came home with Paul. We heard Lou running towards the front door. For the first time he wagged his tail. Then Lilly came running behind him. I bent down on my knees and Lilly licked my face! We were ecstatic. Lou was telling us that he was happy and that he trusted us. It was definitely worth the wait.

It took time to teach them how to walk on leashes and not be afraid of trucks because when they were on the streets alone, they had a lot of close calls. Lilly and Lou probably darted across the streets many times to escape a truck or bus that was coming towards them. I had seen this happen at least twice when I followed them so I knew why they would be terrified. Since Lou wasn't motivated by treats, I had to figure out another way to turn a bad experience into a good one so he could calmly walk outside. As soon as a truck would start coming down the street toward us, I would hold Lou's leash close to me as we stood on the sidewalk. Then I'd get very happy and say, "Lou, look at that huge truck coming toward us. Isn't that a nice truck?"

My voice sounded like I was winning prizes on a game show. Eventually Lou associated the trucks with happiness but he also knew that we needed to stop before we crossed the street. I bet people thought I was a nut job.

When my parent's friend Bob came over to meet Lilly and Lou and to see Bella again, I told him about my game show technique and it made him smile. In his tough New York accent he said, "Well, Alicia, I can't say that I've ever used that technique but it sounds like it has worked. It's definitely another form of positive reinforcement."

I laughed. On the outside Bob looks like the kind of guy you wouldn't want to mess with. The thought of him using my game show thing was pretty funny. He continued, "The important thing is that now Lou is able to walk confidently and calmly on a leash and you achieved this in a positive, kind way. I can tell by how relaxed these three dogs are that you're giving them the respect and care they deserve and they know that you're their pack leader."

Even though Lilly was smaller, she had been the leader on the street. She opened up to us more easily, though she was still cautious. Sometimes it seemed like she was still checking me out. She'd look at me through the corner of her eye. When I saw her do this, I would say to her, "What's up Lilly? Do you trust me yet? Everything's going to be okay."

Sometimes if I had rehearsal after school my mom would walk all three dogs in the park. It would take her a long time to get there and back. She told me that people on the street would stop her and say, "Hey, aren't those the two dogs who were out in the park this winter?"

People gave us money to pay for Lilly and Lou's first visit to the vet. Since we were fostering the dogs and it was pretty expensive, Mom agreed to accept the donations, especially from one very generous and persistent woman. She wasn't able to help with the rescue, but she wanted to contribute in some way. It made this woman so happy to be able to help. But after that, my mom would not let us take any other donations from people.

After a couple of months had passed Mom started asking when this "temporary" situation was going to end.

Bella looked up at her and I know she was thinking ... *Yeah, Alicia, I've been thinking about that too.* It had taken so much time and effort to help Lilly and Lou feel safe that I was afraid for them to be with someone new. Besides, I had fallen madly in love with them.

Lilly and Lou slept huddled together in the same bed since the minute they were in our apartment. These two dogs needed so much love and patience. They needed to be hand fed. I would sit on the ground with them, put the food in my hands and feed them. Lilly and Lou were so polite with each other. Lou would always wait until Lilly had eaten as much as she wanted before he would start to eat. He would do this even though there were two bowls of food in front of them.

In keeping with the plan I made with Mom, I told her that I felt they were well enough adjusted that we could now try to find a "permanent" home for Lilly and Lou even though I wasn't ready for them to go. I met a woman who expressed interest in them. I asked a lot of questions like whether she would take the dogs to the park everyday for exercise and where they would sleep and how she would care for them. She said they would sleep in the kitchen, she would take them out for a couple of quick walks each day and for exercise they could run in her apartment, but she wouldn't have time to take them to the park to run. I knew they would need more exercise than that and they would need to be outside more. I didn't even bother telling my mom about this lady.

Then one day, my mom came back from the park and said she had found the perfect person to take Lilly and Lou. I asked her who it was and told her I'd find the guy in the park the next day. I found him exactly where my mom said he'd be. He seemed like a nice man so I told him the truth. I told him that I didn't really want to give the dogs up and I needed his help. He already knew their story, so he understood why I didn't want to give them up. I asked him to please tell my mom that he had changed his mind and that he could no longer take the dogs. He did not want to get involved in my lie so he said that he wouldn't show up in the park the next day as usual. He suggested that I think of another plan to keep the dogs instead of lying to my mom. He said that I should talk to my mother about my dilemma. "Why not tell her how attached you've grown to them?" he asked. I thought he was making a big deal out of nothing, especially since I was doing the best thing for Lilly and Lou.

I went home that night and told my mom that I had spoken with the guy and that he said he'd make a decision by the next day. When Mom returned from the park the following day she said, "Hmmm, that's strange, he wasn't there."

I told Mom not to worry, and I winked at Lilly and Lou. This happened two more times. Mom would find someone, I would run to the park, talk to them, and then they wouldn't be there when my mom showed up. Only one person helped me with my lie and said that she had a change of heart. I felt bad for fibbing but I was trying to buy time to figure out what to do.

36

I couldn't handle the idea of giving Lilly and Lou away.

Then one day I met a woman in the park who knew the Lilly and Lou story well. She was involved in rescuing other dogs and I liked her a lot. She said she would be interested in adopting Lilly and Lou from us if I wanted. I told her that I had become very attached to them and didn't want to find them another home but agreed that maybe it would be best since I did tell my mother that it was only temporary. I told the woman about my fibs. I'm not sure why I opened up to her but I did. She understood why I would be tempted to do something like that but suggested that I be honest with my mom.

"Lying is just not a good habit to get into in order to get your way," she said.

She was passionate about this and didn't give me a big long lecture. It got me thinking about what I had done and I started to feel weird about not being honest with my mom. But I was attached to these dogs. I sat on a park bench and tried to figure out how I could tell her the truth. I had trouble figuring out what I would say, so I decided I'd just take a deep breath and talk to her. I would let what was on my mind come out. My play director called this improvisation.

As I entered our building, I saw that my favorite doorman Eduardo was on duty at the front desk. Eduardo was a friend to us for all the years we had lived in that building.

"You doing okay, Ms. Alicia?" Eduardo asked. He always seemed to know if I was in a good mood or not. I thought that Eduardo was probably a great dad to his two daughters and one son. I leaned up against the front desk and rested my chin on

my hands and blurted out, "Mr. Morales, I told a lie. Well...
actually, I told one lie, three different times and now I'm scared
to fess up."

His eyes crinkled up when he smiled. "So you really lied
three times even if it was the same one! Either way, it's always
better to tell the truth. Everything will be okay if you do the
right thing. It might not feel good before you do it or right
afterwards either, but in the long run, it's the best choice. And
how many times do I have to tell you to call me Eduardo?"

He made me smile even though my stomach was doing
somersaults anticipating the conversation with my mother.
"Thanks Eduardo."

"De nada, Ms. Alicia." I loved the way his accent made my
name sound.

I got onto the elevator feeling stronger after talking to
Eduardo. I opened the door to our apartment ready to talk to
my mom.

"Mom, Mom," I blurted out from the front door as I
dropped my backpack on the bench. While I was calling her
name, I could hear her shouting, "Alicia, please come here. I
need to talk to you right away."

My heart was in my throat and I couldn't hear anything but
the sound of it thumping. She must have found out that I lied.

Before she could say another word, I begged her, "Mom,
can I please talk to you right away?"

She interrupted me, "Alicia, I have something I really need to say."

I did not want to be rude but I said, "Mom, please I can't stand it anymore." Now my mom seemed alarmed. "What is it? Tell me."

I told her what I had done, apologized and told her I would never betray her trust again. I put my head down. I was afraid to see her reaction. It seemed like a year had passed before she spoke.

Finally I heard her say my name in a way that was not like the voice she uses when I'm in trouble.

"Alicia," she said and reached over to pick up my chin.

I looked up and saw her smiling. "I am not happy that you lied. I'm not happy that you had me going to and from the park like that. But, I am proud of the courage it must have taken to admit what you've done."

She told me how cool she thought it was of me to take time from watching TV or hanging out with my friends so that I could help rescue the dogs and still manage to keep up with school and rehearsal.

I promised her that I would never do anything like that again.

We hugged and I apologized again. "I'm really sorry, Mom."

We both walked into the kitchen to get the dogs' dinner

ready. Before I could get the bowls out for the pups' dinner, my mom reached into the fridge to get some homemade food she had prepared for them earlier. She sat down on the floor and started hand-feeding Lilly and Lou. I continued talking while I fed Bella. I watched my mom feed Lilly and Lou and thought how sad I was going to be when they had to leave us.

Then I said, "Oh I have something else I need to tell you. There was one woman in the park who knows Lilly and Lou and their story. I think she would be able to give them a good home. She's great with dogs. I still don't want to let them go but I did make a promise to you." It was hard for me to look at Lilly and Lou and I didn't want to cry.

My mom waited for Lilly to take one more bite then she looked up at me and said, "Are you crazy? We can't give them away now. Could you please give me some more food?"

I thought I was hearing things. "What did you say, Mom?"

She tilted her head and said, "You can go back to the park tomorrow and thank that woman for the offer, but Lilly and Lou have been officially adopted by us."

I was beyond ecstatic. I started to sing and dance and hug my Mom as hard as I could. We ordered my favorite vegetarian sausage and soy cheese pizza from Viva Pizza on Broadway and had a party.

Eventually Lou, Lilly, Bella and I became known as the four redheads. People would stop and stare at us and say, "Wow, what an interesting group."

Lilly was the smallest. Lou was a bit bigger, Bella was bigger than Lou, I was bigger than Bella, and we all had red hair. They'd look at us and say, "Oh, wow, small, medium, large and extra large."

Before we moved to Los Angeles a little over two years ago, we had a going away party at Riverside Park. I invited the whole rescue team and all the people in the neighborhood who had gotten to know and love them. My mom hired a catering service to come to the park in the morning and serve fresh muffins, bagels, coffee, juice, spring water, and special dog treats. The caterer was confused as to where the party would be.

I heard my mother talking to her on the phone. "Yes, the party is going to be at the dog park at Riverside Park just above Ninety-Eighth Street. You won't be able to miss us." It was cute watching the catering lady hang onto her heavy cart as she trotted down the little hill trying not to lose control of it. One of the guys ran to her to give her a hand. Afterwards, she said that it was the most special party she had ever catered.

My dad was looking forward to our arrival in Los Angeles and he was interested in Lilly and Lou. He'd always ask, "So, what's the latest with the two dogs and are you packed and ready to head west?"

After the going away party, I called him with the update and asked lots more questions. He told me not to worry about putting the dogs on the airplane, especially since my mom had done research on which airline had the best reputation for safely transporting pets. Lilly and Lou would travel in one really big crate and Bella would have her own crate. My dad must have sent out some special sort of wish to the airport because at the check-in line a wonderful man who worked for the airline greeted my mom and me. I think he could see how nervous I was. He said, "Go outside and walk your dogs. Then come back and see me. I will make sure that your dogs are the very last to go onto the plane so that they don't have to stay in cargo too long and when you land in LA, they will be the first ones to get out of cargo."

I wondered if he was an angel. As we were sitting in our seats on the plane, I looked out onto the tarmac and saw the two crates going into the belly of the plane but I felt secure and grateful that this guy helped us. We were on our way to LA with love and good wishes.

*　*　*　*　*

Suddenly I jumped as I heard my cell phone ring. My mom was reminding me that I'd be late for school if I did not get home soon. I looked down. Lilly looked up at me, and I know she was thinking ... *What did I tell you? Jeez, Alicia, you talk, talk, talk, talk, talk.* Then it dawned on me that this kind woman had been so engrossed in the story like me, that we almost forgot where we were.

"How absolutely beautiful, Alicia and it's wonderful that you've given these two such a good home," said Ina.

"I'm not the only one who is good to them." I told her about the two boys who live in the front house on our property and even though they're the toughest guys I've ever met, they are really gentle with Lilly and Lou.

"It's funny, some of the hippest people I've met seem to be the kindest," Ina remarked. "It actually takes a strong person to be kind."

"It looks as though you've shown people how you would like them to treat you and your dogs. That's important," she explained.

Ina continued, "When I was younger and growing up in London, of course that was decades ago, I had a little white French Poodle named Dominique. I simply adored her. Recently I've realized that I had learned many life lessons from my darling Dominique; things like patience, love, enjoying nature and being kind. Your story reminds me of this. It seems as though this has happened to you too. I would have been

43

delighted if someone had shared a story like yours with me when I was young."

"Thanks, Ina. The only bad thing that remains from Lou's past is a scar on his back leg and a little shyness. I look at the scar every now and then to remind myself of the hard life he had." Ina nodded her head and said, "Exactly. We all may have scars whether they are on the inside or the outside. All people and animals have stories and backgrounds and should be treated with kindness, love and respect."

"Wow, that's cool," I said to Ina. I couldn't believe how I had been so focused on her bird landing pad of a hat, electric lipstick and the loud flowers on her dress.

"I'm sorry, love, I took all your time this morning," Ina said.

"Please, I did all the talking. And anyway, I'm so happy when people care and show interest like you do."

Just as we were getting ready to say goodbye, Howie the cool camera man came over to our table. "Excuse me, sorry to interrupt, but are you Ina Weston, the columnist for the West Times Magazine?"

Ina smiled, "Yes, I am."

"I'm Howie. My friends and I were talking about that really funny story you did last week. You're great."

Suddenly, Ina seemed shy.

"Thank you so much, Howie. You are very kind."

She continued, "I just heard a great story from my new friend, Alicia."

Howie looked over at me and smiled.

"I am going to give Alicia my business card and ask her mother to give me a call. I'd like to run this piece in our magazine and open up some avenues for Alicia to tell her tale to groups of young adults. I think there's a lot to learn from this story."

"Nice going Alicia." Howie shook my hand, smiled and said, "How cool is that?"

Ina let out a little chuckle. "Please, I could chatter on all day long. When we meet again, I will tell you more about my little Dominique. I think I've finally recovered from the loss of Dominique and am ready to give my love to another dog. Perhaps you can tell me where the animal shelters are?"

"For sure. I have a list of every animal shelter in the city! If you'd like, I could show you around the one where I volunteer. Adopting from a shelter is definitely the way to go," I assured Ina.

"Well, that would be wonderful, thank you, Alicia," she said.

Just as the waiter put the bill on the table, Ina reached out and grabbed it.

"This was my treat." I went to shake her hand but she gave

me a hug.

"It was really nice to meet you, Ms. Weston. This was a great morning!"

I looked down and smiled at Lilly and Lou who make me and countless others so happy.

"Come on, my precious pups, let's get moving."

ABOUT THE AUTHOR

Doriane Lucia has been formally involved in animal rescue and Humane Education since 1994. While living in New York City, she assisted the ASPCA's Humane Educator with lessons for children. Invaluable experience was also gained while working as an Adoption Counselor at one of the most highly regarded animal shelters in the country.

Doriane is the founder of Humane Nation Foundation through which she creates and conducts Humane Education lessons. She also holds individual consultations bridging the gap between what is legal and what is humane to better the life of a dog, the family and the community.

Doriane received her Master's degree in Humane Education from Cambridge College in Boston, MA and The Institute for Humane Education. She is also a member of APHE (Association for Professional Humane Educators) and received the ASPCA's certificate in Humane Education.

The Story of Lilly & Lou has been introduced to many young adults and children. Doriane thanks you for bringing this story into your home or classroom as it has proven to be a successful tool to help tap into the compassion, potential and passion of our children. A companion workbook with lesson plans is available at:

www.humanenation.us

Mick, Doriane, Sadie and Bula

Printed in the United States
151676LV00001B/3/P